AMAZING MIGRATIONS

ON THE MOVE WITH CHRISTMAS ISLAND RED CRABS

by Rebecca Donnelly
illustrated by Alan Brown

GRASSHOPPER

Tools for Parents & Teachers

Grasshopper Books enhance imagination and introduce the earliest readers to fiction with fun storylines and illustrations. The easy-to-read text supports early reading experiences with repetitive sentence patterns and sight words.

Before Reading

- Discuss the cover illustration. What do readers see?
- Look at the glossary together. Discuss the words.

Read the Book

- Read the book to the child, or have him or her read independently.
- "Walk" through the book and look at the illustrations. Who are the main characters? What is happening in the story?

After Reading

- Prompt the child to think more. Ask: What dangers do Cooper, Carlos, and Caleb encounter on their trip across the island? How do they stay safe?

Grasshopper Books are published by Jump!
5357 Penn Avenue South
Minneapolis, MN 55419
www.jumplibrary.com

Library of Congress Cataloging-in-Publication Data

Names: Donnelly, Rebecca, author.
Brown, Alan, illustrator.
Title: On the move with Christmas Island red crabs
Rebecca Donnelly; illustrated by Alan Brown.
Description: Minneapolis, MN: Jump!, Inc., [2023]
Series: Amazing migrations | Includes index.
Audience: Ages 7-10
Identifiers: LCCN 2021060752 (print)
LCCN 2021060753 (ebook)
ISBN 9781636908823 (hardcover)
ISBN 9781636908830 (paperback)
ISBN 9781636908847 (ebook)
Subjects: LCSH: Chaceon–Christmas Island (Indian Ocean)–Juvenile literature.
Gecarcinidae–Christmas Island (Indian Ocean)–Juvenile literature.
Crabs–Migration–Juvenile literature.
Migratory animals–Juvenile literature.
Classification: LCC QL444.M33 D66 2023 (print)
LCC QL444.M33 (ebook)
DDC 595.3/86–dc23/eng/20220110
LC record available at https://lccn.loc.gov/2021060752
LC ebook record available at https://lccn.loc.gov/2021060753

Editor: Eliza Leahy
Direction and Layout: Anna Peterson
Illustrator: Alan Brown

Printed in the United States of America at Corporate Graphics in North Mankato, Minnesota.

Table of Contents

Across the Island

Hi, I'm Cooper. I'm a Christmas Island red crab. I live in a burrow in the forest.

It's spring here on Christmas Island. It is the rainy season. It's time for us to migrate to the beach.

"Come on, Carlos! Come on, Caleb!" I call to my friends.

There are about 45 million red crabs on this island. Once we're four years old, we migrate to the ocean to mate. The males start first. The females will join us soon. The beach is about two miles (3.2 kilometers) away. It takes us a couple weeks to get there.

"Follow me, guys! This looks like a shortcut!" Caleb says.

"Stop!" says Carlos. "That's where the yellow crazy ants live! They're small but dangerous predators. They spray acid. Let's get out of here!"

Next, the three come across a robber crab.

"Oh, no!" says Carlos. "Their claws can cut right through our shells! This way, guys!"

We march as fast as we can.

“I can see the beach!” says Caleb. “Don’t cross the road! Let’s follow this fence.”

"This bridge goes over the road. We can cross safely here," says Carlos.

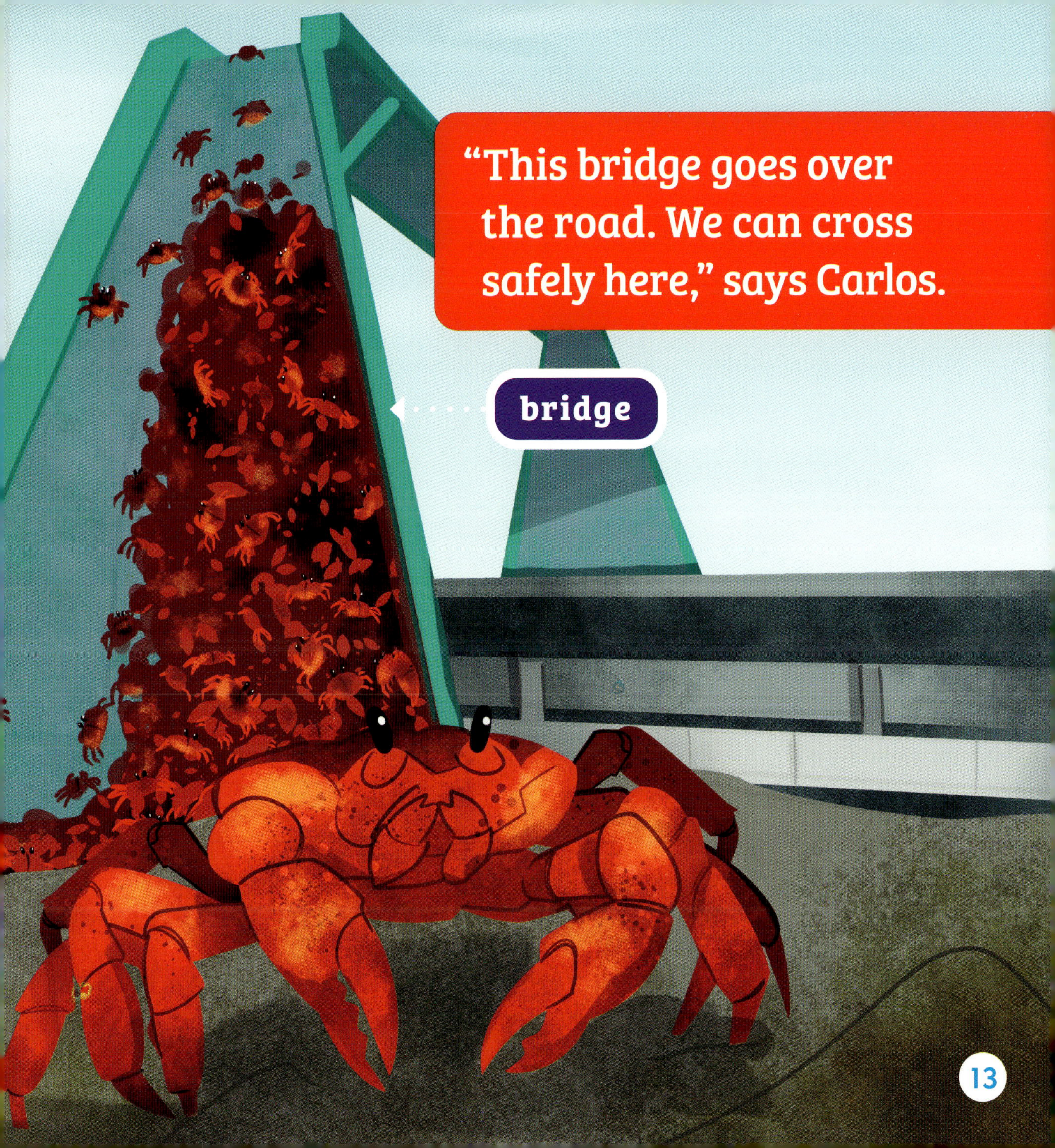

“We made it!” says Caleb.

We get some water after the long trip. Then, we each dig a burrow. When the females come, we’ll mate. After that, the males return to the forest. I hope we don’t run into that robber crab again!

The females wait on the beach for a couple weeks. They each carry about 100,000 eggs! When the tide is high and there's a quarter moon, they will spawn.

They each poke their egg sac with a claw and do a shimmy. This dance releases their eggs into the water.

When crabs hatch, they are called larvae. I remember being a tiny larva. I lived in the ocean for about one month. I was lucky I didn't get eaten by a whale shark! Then, the waves pushed me to shore.

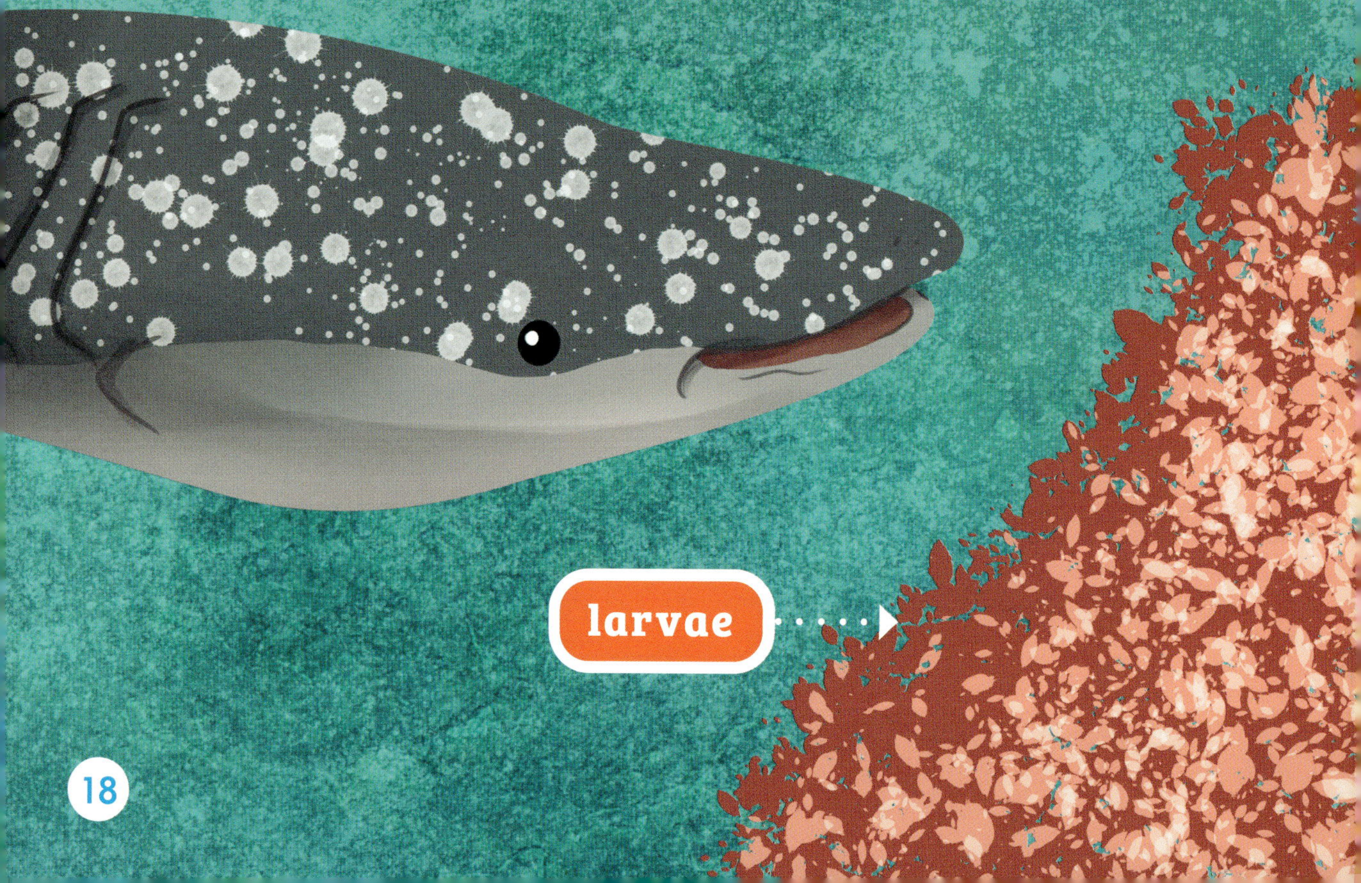

Soon, we molted and became adult crabs. It was our turn to migrate across the island to the forest.

After a few days of marching, Carlos, Caleb, and I arrive home. We have been away for four weeks! We clean up by moving and eating dead leaves.

We'll stay here until it's time to migrate again. See you next year!

Migration Map

Christmas Island is in the Indian Ocean. Christmas Island red crabs migrate from forests to the beach. The journey can take a couple weeks and can be several miles long. Take a look!

= forest = beach = mating area

Let's Review!

Why do Cooper, Carlos, and Caleb migrate from the forest to the beach?

A. to find food **B.** to mate
C. to escape robber crabs **D.** to swim

Glossary

acid: A chemical yellow crazy ants spray to kill red crabs.

burrow: A hole or tunnel in the ground that some animals use as a home.

egg sac: A case that holds the eggs of a female crab and hangs in the water.

hatch: To break out of a shell.

larvae: Young crabs that have just hatched from their eggs.

mate: To join together to produce young.

migrate: To move from one area to another at certain times of the year.

molted: Shed an old shell and replaced it with a new one.

predators: Animals that hunt other animals for food.

shimmy: The movement a female crab makes to release eggs from her egg sac.

spawn: To produce a large number of eggs.

Let's Review! Answer Key: **B.** to mate

Index

To Learn More

Finding more information is as easy as 1, 2, 3.

1. Go to www.factsurfer.com
2. Enter "**onthemovewithChristmasIslandredcrabs**" into the search box.
3. Choose your book to see a list of websites.